MW01048004

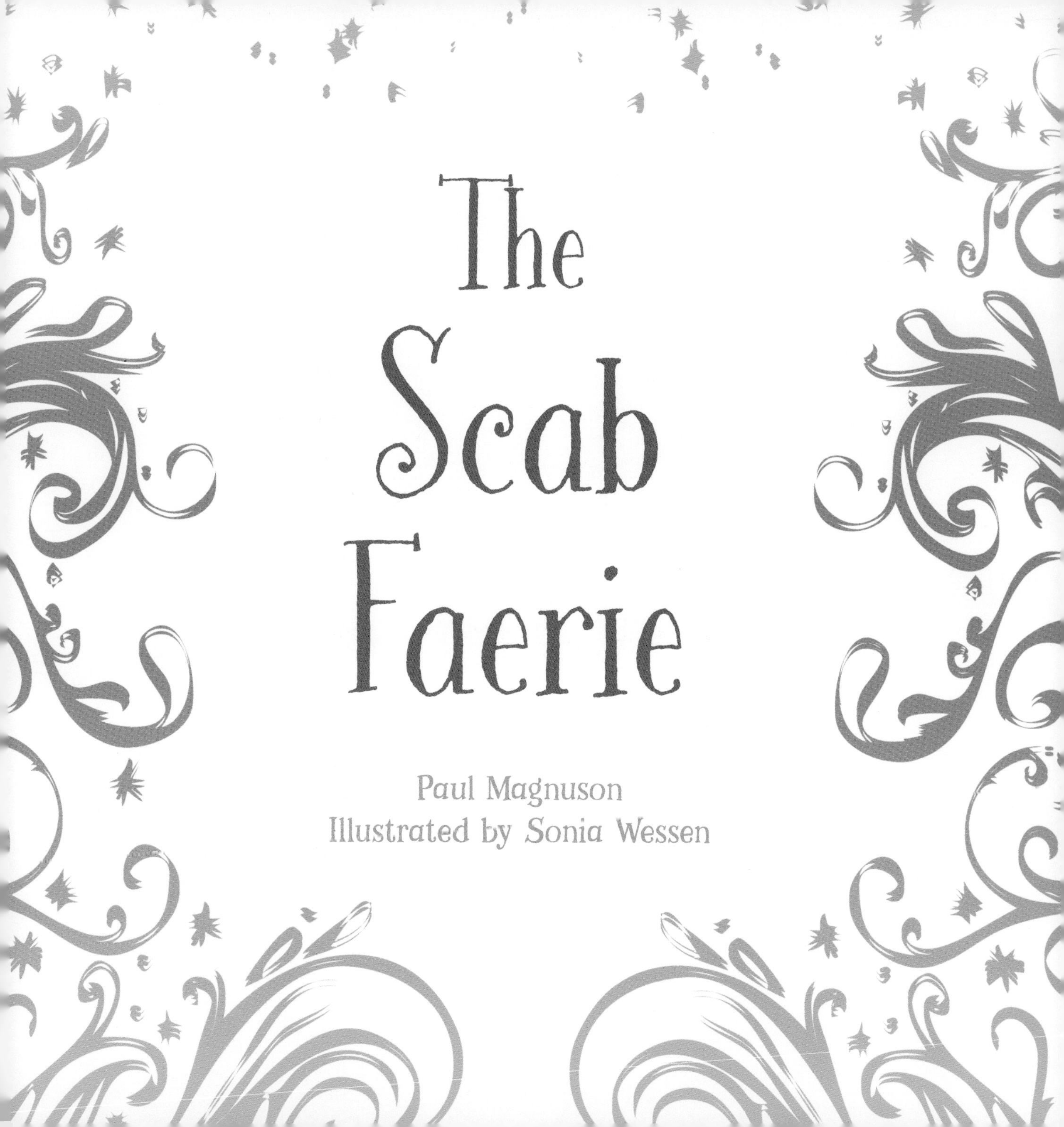

The Scab Faerie

Paul Magnuson
Illustrated by Sonia Wessen

Illustrations by Sonia Wessen
Book design by Laura Drew
Production Editor: Becca Hart

ISBN: 978-1-64343-809-2

Library of Congress Catalog Number: 2020921927

Printed in the United States of America
First Printing: 2021
25 24 23 22 21   5 4 3 2 1

Beaver's Pond Press, Inc.
939 Seventh Street West
Saint Paul, MN 55102

To order, visit
www.magnusonedstudio.ch or
www.BeaversPondPress.com.
Reseller discounts available.

Contact Paul Magnuson at www.magnusonedstudio.ch for school visits, speaking engagements, book club discussions, and interviews.

To all faeries everywhere,
real and imagined,
who are doing their best.
—Paul

To Jia,
my loving sibling and
artistic inspiration.
—Sonia

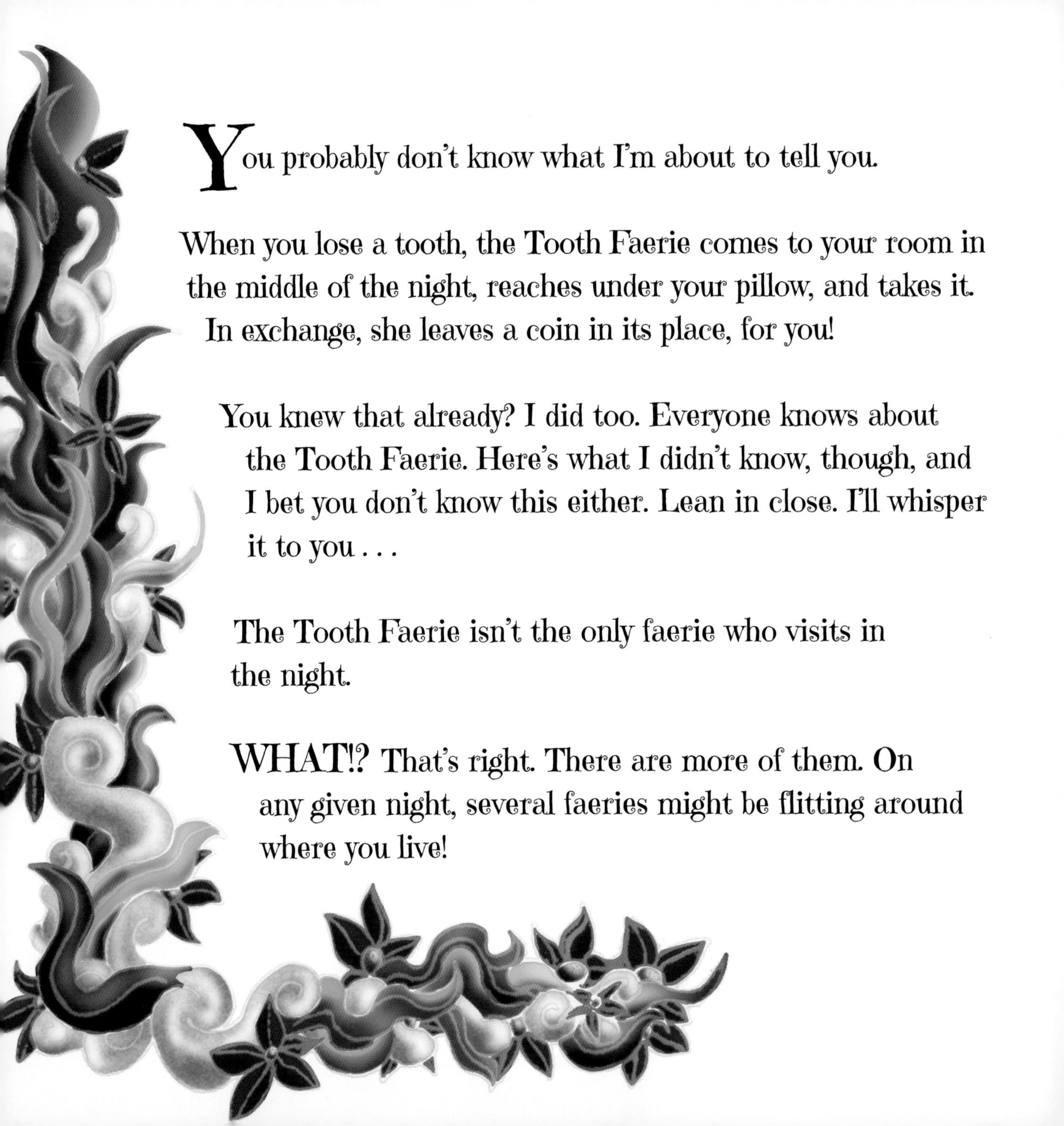

You probably don't know what I'm about to tell you.

When you lose a tooth, the Tooth Faerie comes to your room in the middle of the night, reaches under your pillow, and takes it. In exchange, she leaves a coin in its place, for you!

You knew that already? I did too. Everyone knows about the Tooth Faerie. Here's what I didn't know, though, and I bet you don't know this either. Lean in close. I'll whisper it to you . . .

The Tooth Faerie isn't the only faerie who visits in the night.

WHAT!? That's right. There are more of them. On any given night, several faeries might be flitting around where you live!

Before I tell you about the Scab Faerie (yes, that's one of them, which you probably guessed by the title of this story), I'll prove to you that there are many kinds of faeries.

For example, have you ever been unable to find a matching sock? Yes? It happens to me all the time. It's because of the Sock Faerie. Yes! It's true. He takes just one. It's all he can carry. Faeries are very little, you know.

Have you ever heard your mom or dad say they can't find their keys? They'll say, "I know I left them right here." But the keys aren't there. Why? You guessed it, the Key Faerie. Usually she just moves them somewhere in the house, because keys are really heavy for her, even with her helpers.

That's right, she has helpers. They are called the Key Teeth Faeries, and they hope to be promoted to Tooth Faerie one day. This is where the expression "cutting your teeth," meaning "to get some experience," actually comes from. Really. Believe me.

Wesson 2020
Dream Faerie

And the next time you can't find a toy you've been playing with? Blame the Toy Faerie. Certainly don't blame yourself!

Don't get carried away, though. When one of your parents comes home from work and says, "I think I'm losing my mind," that is definitely not the work of a faerie. There is no Mind Faerie. There is, however, a Mind Gnome. The Mind Gnome hides in the shadows where parents work. This is where the expression "mind numbing" comes from, though it should probably be spelled "mind gnoming."

But back to the story. The Scab Faerie.

The Scab Faerie's job is exactly what you would predict. She collects scabs, those pieces of bumpy, dried up skin that form over cuts and scrapes. It is not a glamorous job, digging around under the bed covers in the dark, collecting scabs. Not the type of job faeries think about as Faerie Children, when they mostly dream about being the Tooth Faerie, the one with the coins, the one who makes children happiest.

Well, once upon a time—were you worried that this story didn't start correctly? It does now—once upon a time, the Scab Faerie, after a particularly tiring night of hauling away crusty awful scabs, hit upon a novel idea.

Why, she thought to herself, couldn't she, too, leave a coin each time she collected a scab? Then the children would adore her the way they adored the Tooth Faerie. She could hardly fall asleep as she thought about her plan for the next night and her future fame among the children of the world.

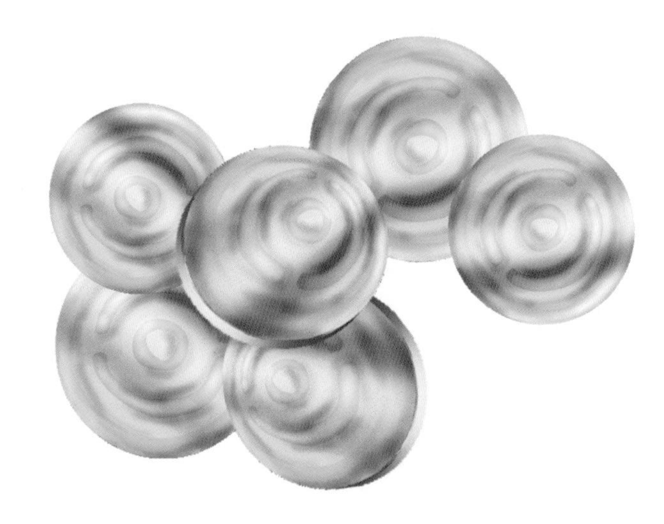

Wessen 2020
Bump in the Night Faerie

That evening, she woke up early, snuck into the Faerie Garden, and stole a leaf of the Magic Mint. The Magic Mint is how the Tooth Faerie makes her coins—that's right, she makes them on the spot, just after collecting a tooth. She takes a teeny-tiny pinch of Magic Mint and rubs it between her finger and thumb to make exactly the right coin. How else would a little faerie carry coins to all the children who have lost teeth? Did you ever consider that?

The Scab Faerie pinched off a piece of Magic Mint for every scab she collected. This is where the term "mint" comes from, by the way, meaning "the big factory where humans make coins." Really. Believe me.

It was a success. The next day, the children were pleasantly surprised by the coins they found in their beds. The Scab Faerie stole another leaf of Magic Mint the next night, and the next, and soon children from far and wide figured out what was going on. When you lose a scab, you get a coin! Just like when you lose a tooth!

At first, the Scab Faerie and the children were very happy with this new arrangement. This is what adults call a "win-win situation," something they say way too often, by the way. It means "two people who are working together both benefit at the same time." In this case, the Scab Faerie was happy that children liked her, and the children were happy, because they could buy candy, or a comic book, or perhaps save some spending money for summer camp. Win-win!

Bleary Eye Faerie

But. (You knew it, didn't you, that there was going to be a *but* somewhere in this story, and I don't mean the kind that you sit on. Please know that there is no faerie related to anything to do with that kind of butt. I can guarantee it. If there were, I would write about it here, because it's a pretty funny thought.)

The Scab Faerie, it turns out, was too successful. Once word had spread across playgrounds that kids could get money for scabs, the accident rate spiked horribly. If you aren't clear what I mean by this, I mean that children started falling down, wiping out, banging their shins, and scraping their knees. They were more than what some adults call "accidents waiting to happen." They were accidents happening, all day long, every day.

It was horrible. And yes, they were also growing scabs, and losing them, and collecting coins, but that only made the Scab Faerie busier and busier, and at the same time encouraged the children to fall from higher and higher heights, take even more dangerous corners with their bikes, and slide into every base, even first base, no matter if they were wearing pants or shorts. (Shorts were even better. More scrapes! More scabs! More coins!)

It didn't take long before parents were very concerned and the other faeries were aware of all the unusual activity. In the end, it was the Sock Faerie who, upon her return one morning, told the Faerie Godmother about all the injuries, all the coins, and her suspicion that the Scab Faerie had gotten into the Magic Mint.

Wessen 2020
Dust Faerie

That same night, the Faerie Godmother was waiting for the Scab Faerie when she returned, utterly exhausted, from her long night of scab collecting. Her wings were frayed, to say nothing of her nerves, and she burst into tears when the Faerie Godmother asked her if she had been stealing the Magic Mint. "Yeeeeeees," she sobbed, frightened, but also relieved to get the whole thing into the open.

Now the Faerie Godmother was not Godmother for nothing. She was experienced and—even better—wise, for wisdom comes with experience for those who keep their eyes open. She explained to the Scab Faerie, patiently, lovingly, that all the faeries have a different role in life, and that all these roles put together is what makes faeries so special.

"Imagine," she told the Scab Faerie, "how cold the feet of the poor humans would be if the Sock Fairy enticed them with coins! Now, now, there, there," she continued. "Everything will be fine."

And thus consoled, the Scab Faerie returned to her coinless past. Within weeks, children gave up trying to grow scabs and were actually happier, because although coins are nice, falling down sort of hurts.

That's the story I wanted to tell you.

And if your parents are having trouble with the Mind Gnome at work, just tell them to read this story with you again tomorrow night, because reading to you is the loveliest way to forget about him. Really. Believe me.

You can see these faeries in the story.
Maybe you have had an encounter with one of them?

DREAM FAERIE

Have you ever had an especially wacky dream that, once you woke up, you just couldn't remember? The Dream Faerie eats dreams for lunch, carefully seeking out the most colorful, vivid, and exciting dreams to add flavor to her meal. It's rumored that drinking warm milk before going to bed gives dreams a pleasant smell, which this faerie really likes, and which ensures a peaceful rest. However, no scientist has yet been able to conclusively replicate these results in the lab.

BUMP IN THE NIGHT FAERIE

This excitable faerie constantly reaches for his own forehead bell, not unlike a pet kitty might chase a string. Unfortunately for humans, he is clumsy and trips over his own big feet, crashing into this and that regularly. The Bump In The Night Faerie has no wings, so he clambers over the floor, tripping and falling as he goes, contributing to the noise of the constantly tinkling bell. The vibrations of movement also set off his other jangling bits, namely his backbone bells and clacking bracelets. He even has a pair of cymbals hidden in his tail!

BLEARY EYE FAERIE

This faerie's eyes are always very dry. She visits homes at night to steal eye-water from everyone in the house, hoping to soothe her itchy eyes. Of course, when she takes our eye-water, we get itchy and crusty eyes. Even worse, she tries on glasses that she finds and leaves them lying just about anywhere in the house. Now, where did I put those glasses?

DUST FAERIE

Have you ever noticed the fine layer of dust on top of shelves and other flat surfaces? Have you ever seen dust floating in the air when the sunlight through the window is just right? Blame the Dust Faerie. Many years ago, she broke her delicate wings in an unfortunate crash. The Faerie Godmother gave her an engine, but her quick-growing hair is constantly trimmed by the blades of the propeller. Now you know where dust really comes from.

MIND GNOME

This grumpy and pessimistic creature is always bored. He likes nothing better than to share his dissatisfaction with others by stretching out time. His other main hobby is growing and taking care of his beard, which should show you just how bored he is. If he ever discovered the existence of children, he'd probably try to bore them instead of adults. Well, good luck. Children's minds are amazing. And besides, parents keep the Mind Gnome far from children by not hiring children at their jobs. Parents sure make a lot of sacrifices for their kids.

These faeries have not been seen often enough for us to verify exactly what they look like, because eyewitness reports tend to contradict each other. If you see one—and if you can add a reliable drawing to the description of their personalities—you can probably get quite famous among those who study faeries. Send your drawings and descriptions to us!

SCAB FAERIE

The Scab Faerie has always been, and probably will always be, very shy. She flies away from pictures as fast as she can. You might see her foot or a bit of a wing in the edge of a picture, but not very often. We thought that if we wrote a whole book about her, someone like you might spot her one night and send us a drawing. It's fun to imagine what she looks like.

Oh wait—she did ask us to tell you this: "Don't pick at those scabs! Your mother is right, let it heal." And: "Don't fall off your bike on purpose. I am **NOT** leaving any coins behind anymore. Besides, the Faerie Godmother won't let me anywhere near the Magic Mint."

TOY FAERIE

The Toy Faerie comes to your house to look for cool toys. He absolutely loves toys. But he is very bad at putting them away when he is done playing. Maybe you've seen evidence that he has visited your house? The Sami of northern Scandinavia regularly report sightings of the Toy Faerie. Some scholars theorize a relation with Christmas Elves.

SOCK FAERIE

The Sock Faerie is notorious for his habit of stealing a single sock out of each pair, in order to teach a lesson to messy children. Maybe that's why his own socks never match. While he might not admit it, he sort of likes the smell of socks, just like many of us sort of like the smell of a farm. Collecting socks makes him feel connected with those large, strange beasts the faeries call "ihmisen," the word they use for "human." Numerous sightings have been reported around the world, yet no reliable image exists.

PHONE FAERIE

The Phone Faerie loves to send texts on any phone she can get into. But like most faeries, the Phone Faerie never learned to spell. Faeries never go to more than one year of school, and all they learn is flying, telling knock-knock jokes, making chocolate-chip cookies, and other worthwhile things. That means their text messages never make sense. Her most famous one is the simple word "Covfefe," but she has a long list of credits to her name. Maybe you have an example?

CRUMB FAERIE

The Crumb Faerie is a second cousin once removed of the Dust Faerie. If you don't know what a second cousin is, nor how one can be "once removed," put your parents on the spot by asking them for an example in ten seconds or less. Owen Lewis and his mother, Mrs. Megan Lewis, reported a sighting of the Crumb Faerie in 1994, in Aberystwyth, Wales. No corroborating sightings were reported.

BAD BREATH FAERIE

There have been numerous reports of the Bad Breath Faerie, the little prankster who squirts a tiny film of Yuck-Smell into any mouth that's open while sleeping. The most famous reports were between 2008 and 2012 by a retired dentist in Katowice, Poland. There's a small statue of Dr. Lech Smierdzacy, DDS, in the city park.

SLEEPWALKING FAERIE

A family in Pacific Grove, California, spoke on a radio talk show about a small being in lime-green overalls who repeatedly escorted them through the front door and onto the lawn while they were sleeping. Because they were asleep every time this happened—that's the nature of sleepwalking, after all—researchers at the University of Santa Cruz were never able to rule out dreaming as the true source of the faerie.

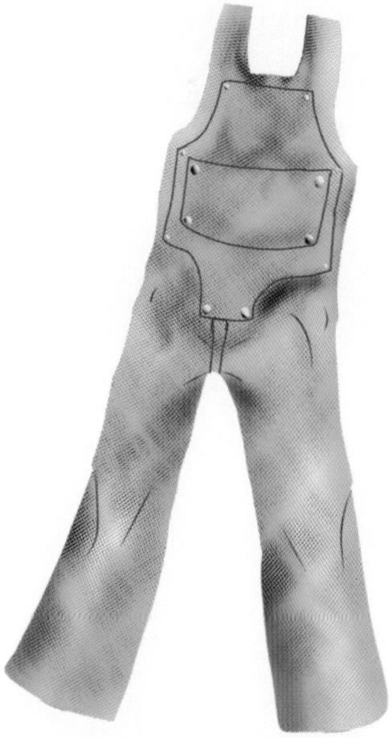

Dear Parents,

We invite you to help young readers imagine what the Scab Faerie looks like. Spread out the drawing supplies and let your child's imagination run wild.

Of course, there are all sorts of faeries not even mentioned in this story, including those who might be visiting your house. Perhaps your child can imagine a faerie that we haven't heard of yet?

Visit www.magnusonedstudio.ch to see our readers' drawings for a little inspiration . . . and to submit a piece of artwork from the faerie finder in your house!

ABOUT THE AUTHOR

Paul Magnuson is a teacher and educational researcher who likes nothing better than word play, creative students, languages, happy children, and improbable explanations for mundane things. He lives in Switzerland with his wife, daughters, and dog, Gilligan. To learn more about Paul and his work, visit www.magnusonedstudio.ch.

ABOUT THE ILLUSTRATOR

Sonia Wessen studies two-dimensional, three-dimensional, and digital art at St. Olaf College, located in Northfield, Minnesota. She uses art to expand the aesthetic imagination with technical skill fit for an adult and raw creativity fit for a child. *The Scab Faerie* is her first experience working on a book.